Milly Molly®

B O O K S

This Milly, Molly book belongs to

_____

For my grandchildren
Thomas, Harry, Ella and Madeleine.

Milly, Molly and Different Dads

Copyright © Milly Molly Books, 2002

Gill Pittar and Cris Morrell assert the moral right to
be recognised as the author and illustrator of this work.

Published by
Milly Molly Books
P O Box 539
Gisborne, New Zealand
email: books@millymolly.com

Printed by Rhythm Consolidated Berhad, Malaysia

ISBN: 1-877297-29-1

10   9   8   7   6   5   4   3   2   1

Milly, Molly
and
Different Dads

"We may look different
but we feel the same."

It was a cold, wet, winter morning.
Miss Blythe asked everyone to take off
their wet shoes and put them by the heater.

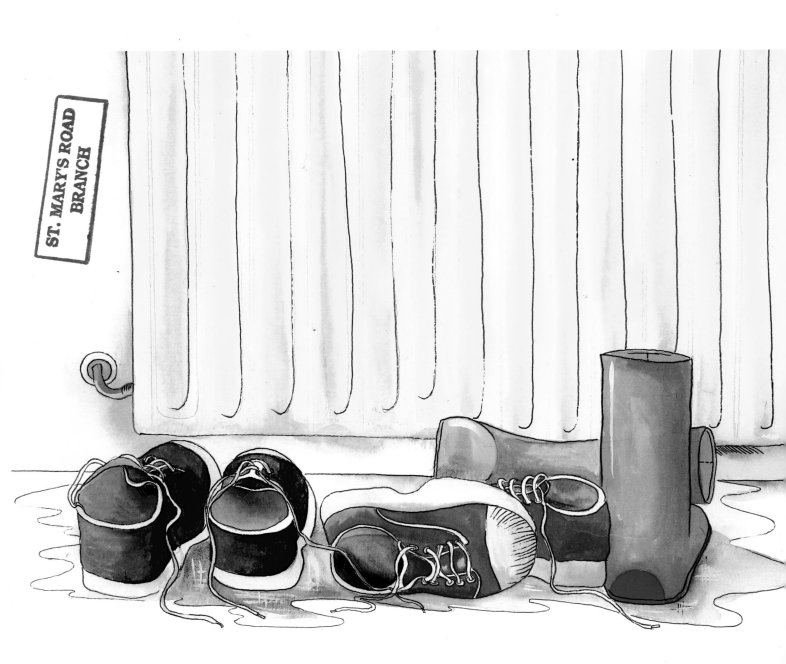

"Come on, let's get warm," she said,
rubbing her hands firmly together.

No one had missed Sophie until, slowly,
the door opened.

Sophie stood dripping. It was hard to tell whether her face was wet with tears or raindrops.

"Come here, Sophie," Miss Blythe said gently.
"Let's take off your wet coat and shoes."

"Can you tell us what's happened?"

"Dad packed his suitcase and left home," sobbed Sophie.

Miss Blythe held Sophie against her warm cardigan and said softly, "Let's talk about our Dads."

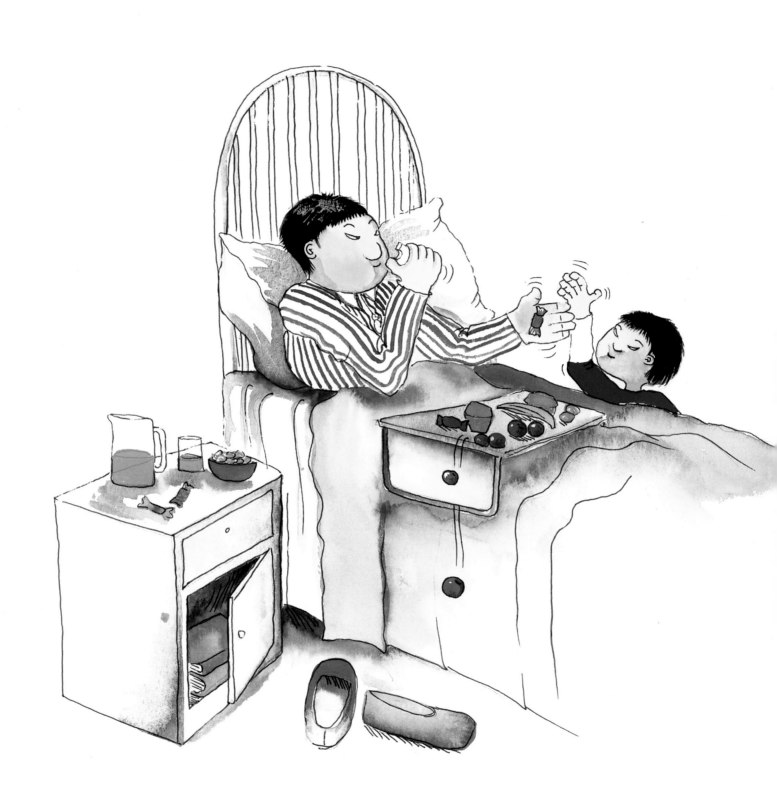

"My Dad's in hospital," started Jack.

"I've got two Dads," said Elizabeth.

"I've only got one Dad," said Milly.

"My Dad's away with the Army and I only
see him sometimes," Harry added.

"My Dad's at home every day," slipped in Tom.

"I go and stay with Dad for holidays because he has another family now," said Poppy.

"My Dad's in a wheelchair," stated Humphrey.

"Dad adopted me when I was one," said Molly.

"Uncle Stan looks after me like a Dad," added George thoughtfully.

"My Dad is blind," said Meg.

"Dad died last year," Alf said quietly.

"And my Dad died when I was six,"
confided Miss Blythe.

Sophie squeezed in between Milly and Molly.

"My Dad is deaf," she said softly.

"So there we are," Miss Blythe said.
"All Dads and families are different.
That's just the way it is."

B O O K S

Other picture books in the Milly, Molly values series include:

- Milly Molly's Monday   ISBN 0-9582208-0-8
- Milly Molly and What Was That?   ISBN 0-9582208-1-6
- Milly Molly and Jimmy's Seeds   ISBN 0-9582208-2-4
- Milly Molly and Beefy   ISBN 0-9582208-3-2
- Milly, Molly and Taffy Bogle   ISBN 0-9582208-4-0
- Milly, Molly and Oink   ISBN 0-9582208-5-9
- Milly, Molly and BushBob   ISBN 0-9582208-6-7
- Milly, Molly and Grandpa's Oak Tree   ISBN 0-9582208-7-5

- Milly, Molly and the Sunhat   ISBN 1-877297-23-2
- Milly, Molly and Alf   ISBN 1-877297-24-0
- Milly, Molly and Aunt Maude   ISBN 1-877297-25-9
- Milly, Molly and Sock Heaven   ISBN 1-877297-26-7
- Milly, Molly and the Secret Scarves   ISBN 1-877297-27-5
- Milly, Molly and the Mountain   ISBN 1-877297-28-3
- Milly and Molly Go Camping   ISBN 1-877297-30-5

www.millymolly.com